Plumbers

A Level Three Reader

By Charnan Simon

Content Adviser: Joseph A. Albergo,
Assistant to the Executive Director,
Council of Chicagoland

The
Child's
World®

Published by The Child's World®

P.O. Box 326
Chanhassen, MN 55317-0326
800-599-READ
www.childsworld.com

Photo Credits
© Christopher Bissell/GettyImages: 6
© Jeff Greenberg/PhotoEdit: 22
© Jim Craigmyle/CORBIS: 21
© Jon Feingersh/CORBIS: 29
© Lester Lefkowitz/CORBIS: 3
© Michael Newmann/PhotoEdit: 10, 13
© Royalty Free/CORBIS: 17, 18, 26
© Romie Flanagan: cover, 9, 14
© Tom Carter/PhotoEdit: 25
© Tony Freeman/PhotoEdit: 5

Editorial Directions, Inc.: E. Russell Primm and Emily J. Dolbear, Editors;
Alice K. Flanagan, Photo Researcher

The Child's World®: Mary Berendes, Publishing Director

Library of Congress Cataloging-in-Publication Data
Simon, Charnan.
  Plumbers / by Charnan Simon.
    p. cm. — (Wonder books)
Summary: An introduction to plumbers and the work that they do.
  ISBN 1-56766-471-7
1. Plumbing—Vocational guidance—Juvenile literature. 2. Plumbers—Juvenile literature.
[1. Plumbers. 2. Occupations. 3. Plumbing.] I. Title. II. Series: Wonder books (Chanhassen, Minn.)
  TH6124 .S53 2003
  696'.1'023—dc21   2002151411

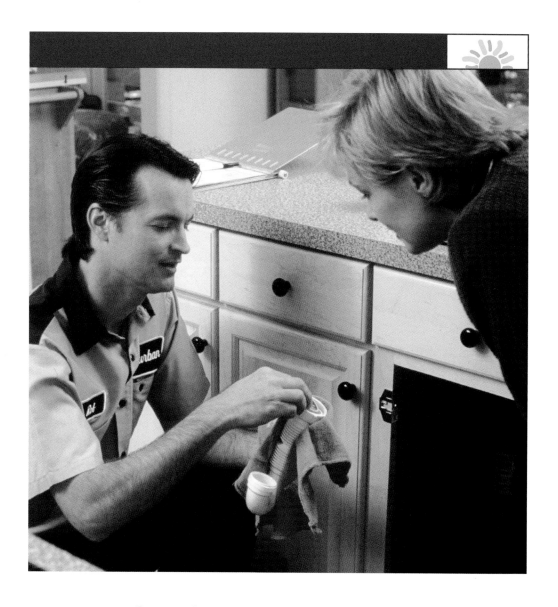

Has a plumber ever visited your home? Plumbers can help fix lots of problems around the house.

Plumbers work with—**plumbing!** Plumbing is the system of water pipes in a building. Some pipes carry clean water into buildings. Some pipes carry dirty water out of buildings.

This plumber works with water pipes. →

Plumbers fix and clean and put in all kinds of pipes. They work on sinks and bathtubs. They also work on washing machines and toilets. Plumbers work with anything that brings water into or out of a building.

Uh-oh! This sink is **clogged**. The water will not flow down the **drain**. Plumbers use a special tool called a snake to unclog the drain. A snake is a special tool made out of thick wires. It fits down drains to clear out the pipe.

A special tool called a snake helps clear the drain. →

9

The pipe under this kitchen sink has a leak. Leaky pipes waste water. It's time for the plumber to fix the pipe with her **wrench**.

This plumber uses a wrench under the sink.

Plumbers don't just fix things that are broken. They also put in new **fixtures**, such as sinks, toilets, and bathtubs. They hook up washing machines, dishwashers, and even hot tubs!

A plumber works on the pipes for a new bathtub. →

13

A family is getting a new bathroom sink. The plumber uses a pipe cutter to make the pipe the right length. She is careful to fit everything together just right.

A pipe cutter makes the pipes the right length.

Plumbers use a lot of tools in their work. They keep their tools in a van or truck. They can drive wherever they are needed.

A plumber sits in the back of his van. →

Fixing pipes can be dirty work. Many plumbers wear **overalls** to keep their other clothes clean. They carry a toolbox or wear a tool belt.

This plumber wears overalls and carries a toolbox.

It takes about five years to learn to be a plumber. New plumbers learn by working with master plumbers. Master plumbers have many years of experience. If you like to fix things and work with tools, you might make a good plumber.

A master plumber teaches a new plumber. →

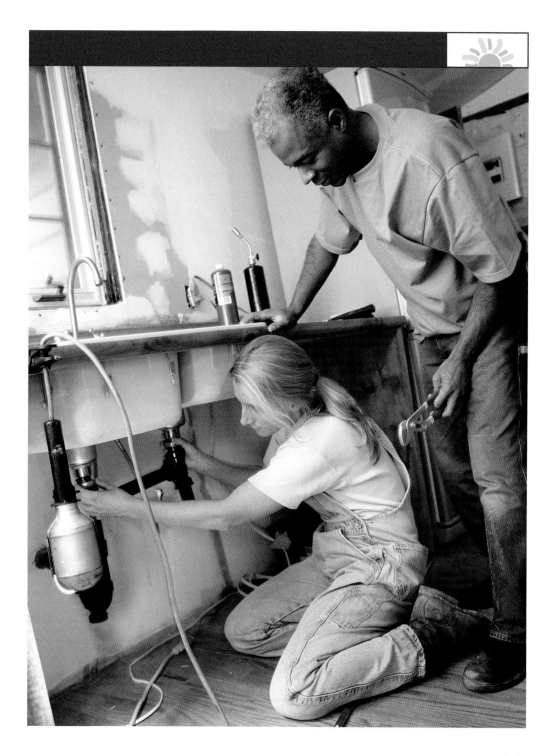

Some plumbers work in homes and apartment buildings. They crawl under sinks. They go down into basements. They might even have to break into walls to fix pipes.

These plumbers fix water pipes in an apartment building.

Some plumbers work outside.
They put pipes into new houses
and buildings. They help build
swimming pools and fountains.

This plumber works on a water pipe outside. →

Did you ever wonder where water from your sink or bathtub or toilet goes? It goes down into the **sewer**. Sewers are big underground pipes that carry away dirty or used water. Plumbers fix sewers, too.

Workers move a sewer pipe.

Plumbers are busy people. They work hard to make sure clean water comes into our houses. They work hard to make sure dirty or used water goes out of our houses. Plumbers are important!

Glossary

clogged (KLOGD)
A clogged bathtub has a blocked drain.

drain (DRAYN)
A drain is a pipe that carries away dirty or used water.

fixtures (FIKS-churs)
Fixtures are things that are put in place to stay.

overalls (OH-vur-allz)
Overalls are a one-piece outfit that fits over other clothes to keep them clean.

plumbing (PLUHM-ing)
Plumbing is the system of water pipes in a house or building.

sewer (SOO-ur)
A sewer is an underground pipe that carries away dirty or used water.

wrench (RENCH)
A wrench is a tool used to tighten or loosen pipes.

Index

To Find Out More

Books

Endersby, Frank. *Plumber: All in a Day.* West Orange, N.J.: Child's Play, 1981.

Lillegard, Dee, and Wayne Stoker. *I Can Be a Plumber.* Chicago: Childrens Press, 1987.

Thomas, Mark. *A Day with a Plumber.* Danbury, Conn.: Children's Press, 2001.

Web Sites

Visit our homepage for lots of links about plumbers:
http://www.childsworld.com/links.html

Note to Parents, Teachers, and Librarians:
We routinely verify our Web links to make sure they're safe, active sites—so encourage your readers to check them out!

Note to Parents and Educators

Welcome to Wonder Books®! These books provide text at three different levels for beginning readers to practice and strengthen their reading skills. Additionally, the use of nonfiction text provides readers the valuable opportunity to *read to learn*, not just to learn to read.

These leveled readers allow children to choose books at their level of reading confidence and performance. Nonfiction Level One books offer beginning readers simple language, word choice, and sentence structure as well as a word list. Nonfiction Level Two books feature slightly more difficult vocabulary, longer sentences, and longer total text. In the back of each Nonfiction Level Two book are an index and a list of books and Web sites for finding out more information. Nonfiction Level Three books continue to extend word choice and length of text. In the back of each Nonfiction Level Three book are a glossary, an index, and a list of books and Web sites for further research.

State and national standards in reading and language arts emphasize using nonfiction at all levels of reading development. Wonder Books® fill the historical void in nonfiction material for primary grade readers with the additional benefit of a leveled text.

About the Author

Charnan Simon lives in Madison, Wisconsin, with her husband and two daughters. She began her publishing career in the children's book division of Little, Brown and Company, and then became an editor of *Cricket Magazine*. Simon is currently a contributing editor for *Click Magazine* and an author with more than 40 books to her credit. When she is not busy writing, she enjoys reading, gardening, and spending time with her family.